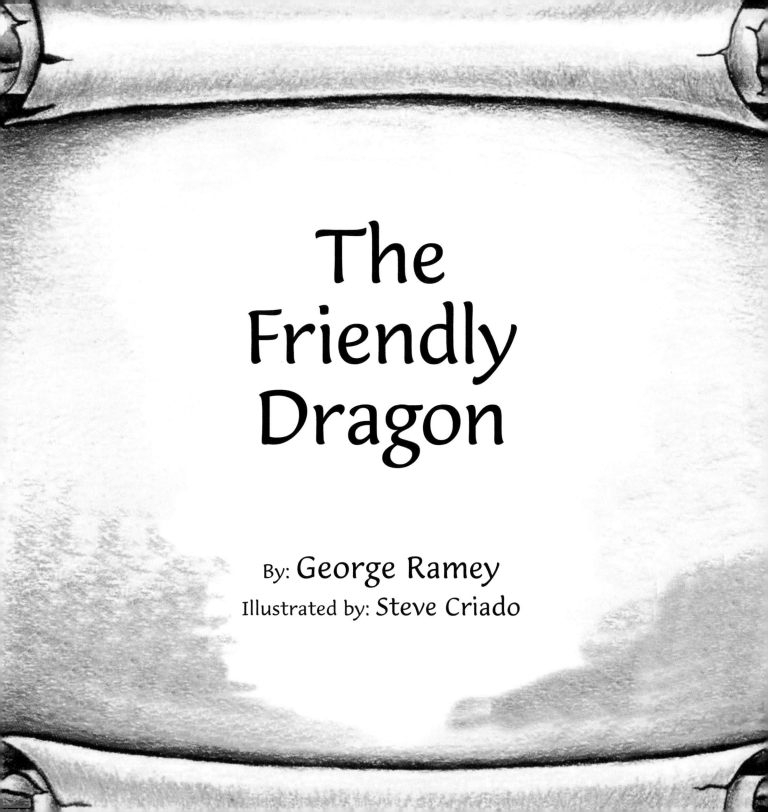

The Friendly Dragon

By: George Ramey

Illustrated by: Steve Criado

AuthorHouse™
1663 Liberty Drive
Bloomington, IN 47403
www.authorhouse.com
Phone: 833-262-8899

This book is printed on acid-free paper.

ISBN: 978-1-6655-1578-8 (sc)
978-1-6655-1579-5 (e)

Print information available on the last page.

Published by AuthorHouse 01/30/2021

authorHOUSE®

Hobby's

My hobby's include writing stories, reading books, writing movie scripts, teaching, and watching sports.

Dedication

What inspired me was all the Authors that wrote the Fairy tale stories, that I grew up on. Also all the children books authors. My three children, Heather George Jr., and Brittany Ramey.

I would like to thank JR Harris from AuthorHouse for their hard work and dedication in publishing my book. My family and friends, for their support. All the children book Authors, for their inspiration, and God for blessing me and my family with this book.

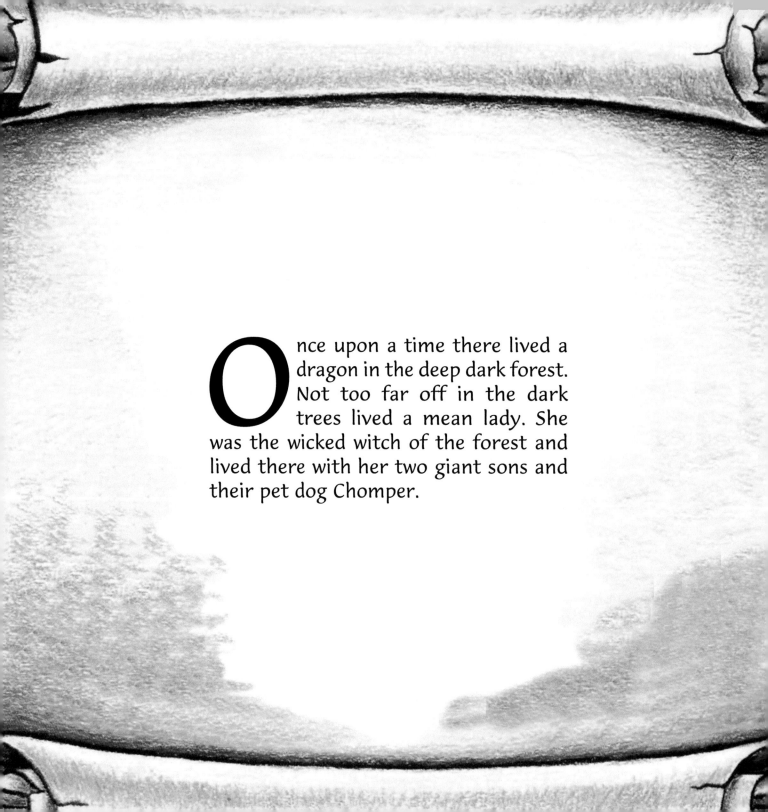

Once upon a time there lived a dragon in the deep dark forest. Not too far off in the dark trees lived a mean lady. She was the wicked witch of the forest and lived there with her two giant sons and their pet dog Chomper.

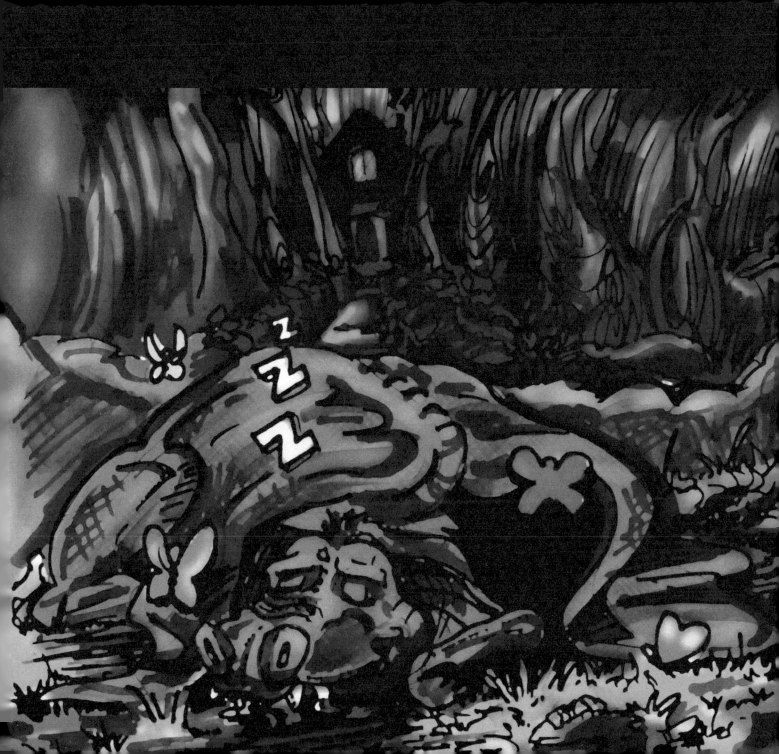

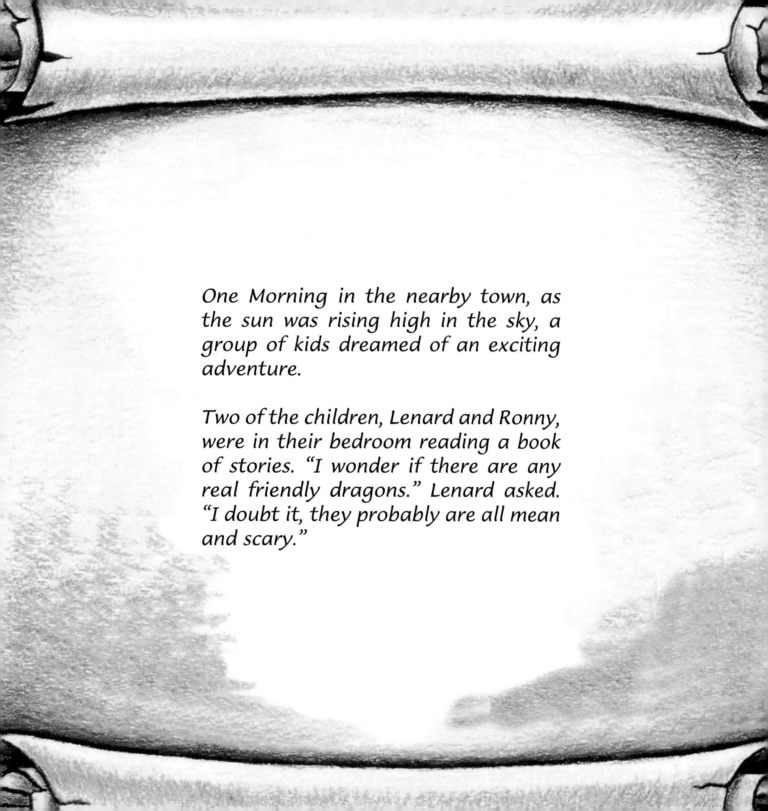

One Morning in the nearby town, as the sun was rising high in the sky, a group of kids dreamed of an exciting adventure.

Two of the children, Lenard and Ronny, were in their bedroom reading a book of stories. "I wonder if there are any real friendly dragons." Lenard asked. "I doubt it, they probably are all mean and scary."

The other two children were playing paddy cake. Sara and K1m are also thinking of dragons. "Boy, I wish that we could go .on an adventure." said Sara. "Let's go tell the boys and see if they have any ideas." Said. Kim. • ·

Sara and Kim went to see if Lenard and; Ronny would want to go on an exciting adventure in the deep dark woods. All the: kids agreed, and they prepared everything that they would need to go 1nto the woods. They brought sandwiches, cookies, chocolate cake, candy and other things they would need. Ronny brought his tent that he and his dad used for camping. They would set up the tent as the1r castle in a clearing in the deep dark woods.

The kids were in the tent when they heard a loud breathing sound. "Let's see what that could be." said Lenard. "Maybe it's just the wind, silly." Laughed Sara. "That's all." The children went outside to find out what the sound was. Their adventure was about to begin . . .

"It's a snoring DRAGON!!!" Squeaked Kim. She didn't want to wake the sleeping dragon. To the children's amazement was a real dragon behind the bushes next to the castle tent. They slowly turned around and at first tippey-toe'd then tried to run away which woke the sleeping dragon. "Don't go!" said the dragon. "I'm a friendly dragon!"

"Stop running!" yelled Lenard, "it's trying to tell us something." They all stopped·and walked back to the dragon, in the deep dark forest. "So what is a dragon doing in the deep dark forest?" asked Sara, "It's not like you can fly free in the trees." The dragon smiled and looked around. "I am trapped here by a mean old lady, she chained me to this tree and I can't fly away," The kids looks at the shackles on the dragon's legs. "Oh no, we've got to get you out of them," yelled Kim. "Yeah, we all have to help you!" everyone said. The dragon was surprised, "No one has helped me, and everyone that sees me laughs and leaves me alone... Thank you children, thank you so much." So the children sat down and thought of a way to get the friendly dragon out of the chains, to a tree in the deep dark forest.

At around that time, the old witch was in her home cooking an icky stew. "Dinner time!" yelled the mean old lady. Running up the hill were her two giant sons Varth and Bolo and their pet dog Chomper. "Mama, mama we found candy wrappers and little footprints on one of the trails!" Varth cried. Bolo came crashing through the door, "yeah yeah yummy kids, candy wrappers, yeah yeah!" The mean old lady in the deep dark forest was thinking of an evil plan. "We'll get the little kiddies, no one escapes my forest!"

"So here's the plan. " Lenard looked up at the tree where the chains led up to. "If we help each other up the tree we can pull the pin that is holding the rope chain. And then our new friend will be free." Everyone thought about it for a second and applauded the idea. "Great idea!" said everyone including the dragon. So the children all line up and hoisted each other up the tree. "If we all work together we can pull this pin out and free our friend." Lenard, Kim, Ronny and Sara helped each other and pulled out the pin.

"Yeah!, your free!" yelled all the kids as they helped each other off the tree. The dragon was so happy to finally be free. She jumped for joy!!! "Thank you children so much! I am free to fly home. Away from this deep dark forest and into the bright beautiful sky!" The dragon spread its wings and started to stretch them out. "It's been so long, I owe each and everyone one of you, you are all so kind to me, and I will never forget you. " The children were so happy that they helped the dragon they all hugged her. "My name is Windy, Windy of the friendly dragon. We are hard to hard to find but are magical. Because you all saved me and given me freedom from these chains I will help you whenever you say my name. No matter how many times, I am forever here for you. I must go now to see my family, they have missed me."

The children were very sad to see their new friend go. "We'll miss you Windy" The children cried, they did not want to finish their adventure. The dragon shared their tears and started to leave, "remember to say my name when you want me to come." And as the dragon flew away the children waved her off into the sunset.

"We better get home, I'm hungry… we shouldn't have eaten all our food and candy," grumbled Ronny. And they made it back to the castle tent and pack things up to take home.

The kids heard the giant footsteps, and came out of the castle to see the two goofy brothers trying to sneak up to the tent. "Get the kiddies!" yelled Varth. The kids ran out away from the tent. "Let's get out of here!" screamed Kim and Sara. The children ran for a second and realized they didn't know, where they were going; the candy wrappers that they left were gone. Just then the giants scooped up the lost children by using the castle tent. The children were captured and the two goofy giants were taking them back to the mean old witch in the deep dark forest.

Back in the mean old lady's house the giant's crash through the door. "We got the kiddies... We got the kiddies...we got the.." "Be quiet!" yelled the mean old lady, "good job, we'll put them in the room for now." The wicked old lady said in her raspy voice. Bolo untied the tent bag and sat the children down. "Are we going to have them for dinner? Yeah yeah dinner?" The mean old lady swung around, "No we're going to use them to build my new castle, throw them in the room and lock the door!" cackled the mean old witch. The children were tossed into a bedroom that looked like a dungeon, there were bars across the windows and no beds to sleep in. "Are we ever going to get out of here? I'm hungry." Cried Ronny. Lenard looked at Ronny "we were almost going to be dinner; we've got to figure a way to get out of here." The children sat down on the cold floor and thought for a second, "I know! They all yelled, we'll call Windy the friendly dragon!"

Windy- was enjoying the sun above the clouds in the mountains. Then she heard the children call her name. She knew now what she had to do.

The boys had managed to open up a crawl space they had found in the dark corner. "Hurry girls, we have an escape" Ronny yelled. Outside of the house the kids gathered their things and started to run. Just then Chompers jumped from the bushes and scared the k1ds. Chompers kept the kids busy while the giant sons and the mean old witch caught up. "Ha ha ha we got you!" said the mean old lady. "We're doomed." Lenard sadly said.

Just then there was a huge shadow over the kids and the mean old witch and the giants. "What's that?" asked Varth. "It's, it's a dragon!" Varth stutters in fear. Bolo starts to run, as Varth grabs a big rock and throws it at the dragon, but misses. The huge dragon kicks up enough wind to help the children escape

"Windy!!! You came back for us!" the children yelled in excitement. The dragon flew down and landed between the kids and the mean old lady. "I am staying here, you guys escape." The children ran as fast as their little legs can go. Over the old castle tent site, down through the trails, through the fence and down the road all the way home.

"I wonder if the dragon made it?" asks Sara. The kids all felt a sigh of relief. They are happy they are safe at home. It was getting dark and they had finally finished their adventure. Out across the sky; over the deep dark forest they saw Windy flying out and into the setting sun. They all talked about the amazing journey they had just went on. They all know that they have a friend with Windy and she returned the favor of rescuing them. As they laughed at the fun they had they all knew that what they had seen was once in a lifetime. "Boy, this was one adventure that we will never forget." Kim said. Everyone agreed and turned in for a very well deserved sleep.

Sketches

Sketches

Sketches

Sketches

Sketches

Sketches

Sketches

Sketches

Sketches

Printed in the United States
By Bookmasters